Dear Parents:

Congratulations! Your child is taking the first steps on an exciting journey. The destination? Independent reading!

STEP INTO READING® will help your child get there. The program offers five steps to reading success. Each step includes fun stories and colorful art or photographs. In addition to original fiction and books with favorite characters, there are Step into Reading Non-Fiction Readers, Phonics Readers and Boxed Sets, Sticker Readers, and Comic Readers—a complete literacy program with something to interest every child.

Learning to Read, Step by Step!

Ready to Read   Preschool–Kindergarten
• big type and easy words • rhyme and rhythm • picture clues
For children who know the alphabet and are eager to begin reading.

Reading with Help   Preschool–Grade 1
• basic vocabulary • short sentences • simple stories
For children who recognize familiar words and sound out new words with help.

Reading on Your Own   Grades 1–3
• engaging characters • easy-to-follow plots • popular topics
For children who are ready to read on their own.

Reading Paragraphs   Grades 2–3
• challenging vocabulary • short paragraphs • exciting stories
For newly independent readers who read simple sentences with confidence.

Ready for Chapters   Grades 2–4
• chapters • longer paragraphs • full-color art
For children who want to take the plunge into chapter books but still like colorful pictures.

STEP INTO READING® is designed to give every child a successful reading experience. The grade levels are only guides; children will progress through the steps at their own speed, developing confidence in their reading.

Remember, a lifetime love of reading starts with a single step!

DISNEY
MOANA

Moana's
Story Collection

Step into Reading, Random House, and the Random House colophon are registered trademarks of Penguin Random House LLC.

Visit us on the Web!
StepIntoReading.com
rhcbooks.com

Educators and librarians, for a variety of teaching tools, visit us at RHTeachersLibrarians.com

ISBN 978-0-7364-4360-9 (trade)

MANUFACTURED IN CHINA
10 9 8 7 6 5 4 3 2 1

DISNEY
M@ANA

Moana's Story Collection

Step 2 and 3 Books

A Collection of Five Early Readers

Random House 🏠 New York

Contents

Moana is brave.

She loves adventure.

She dreams of sailing

the seas.

Maui is a demigod.
He is super strong.

He helps Moana on
her quest!

Maui can change
his shape!

He can be a bug.

He can be a pig.

He can be
a hawk.

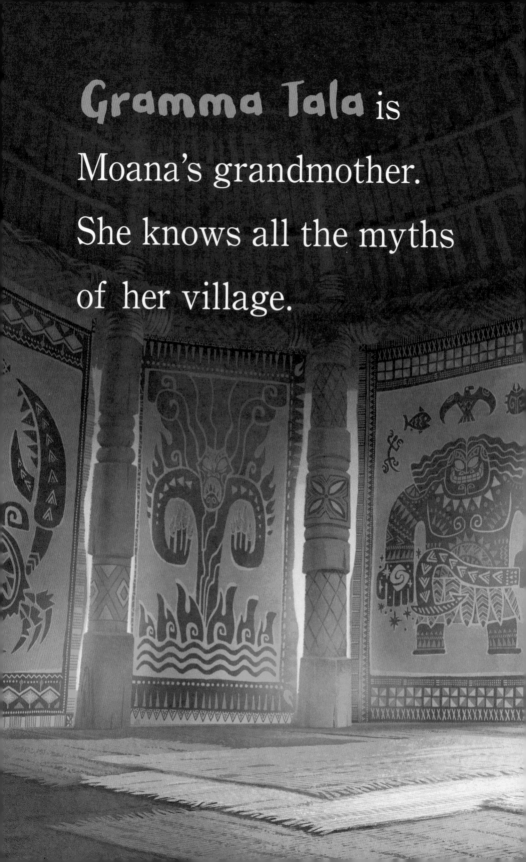

Gramma Tala is Moana's grandmother. She knows all the myths of her village.

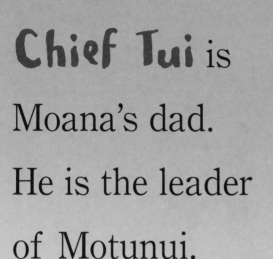

Chief Tui is
Moana's dad.
He is the leader
of Motunui.

He wants to keep
everyone safe.

Sina is Moana's mom.
She loves her family
and her village.

Pua is a pig.
He is Moana's
best friend.
He likes sailing with
Moana.

Heihei is a rooster.

He is very silly!

He does not like the sea.

DISNEY
M@ANA

Moana
Finds the Way

by Susan Amerikaner

illustrated by the Disney Storybook Art Team

Random House 🏠 New York

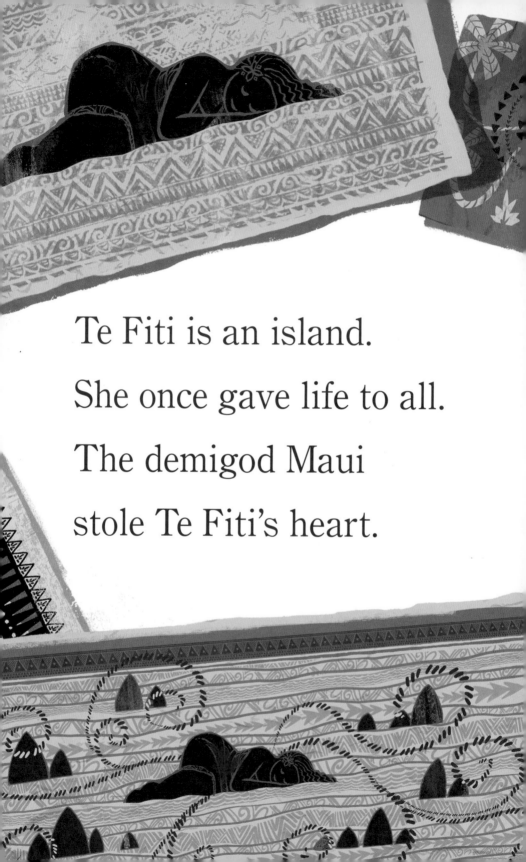

Te Fiti is an island.

She once gave life to all.

The demigod Maui

stole Te Fiti's heart.

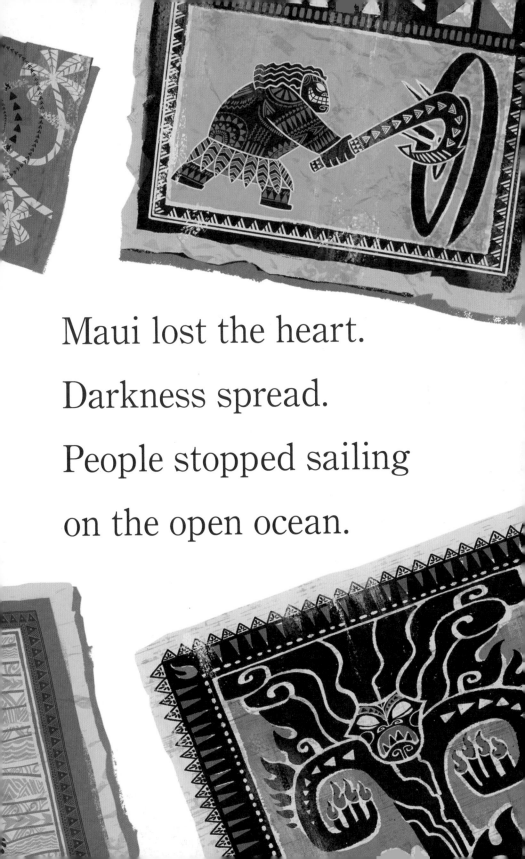

Maui lost the heart.

Darkness spread.

People stopped sailing
on the open ocean.

Moana lives
on an island.
She loves the ocean.

It gives her a shiny gift.

It is the heart of Te Fiti!

Moana grows up.
Gramma Tala shows her
a cave full of boats.
Moana's people once
loved to sail!

Moana thinks she would
love to sail, too.

Gramma Tala tells Moana
she must find Maui
and return Te Fiti's heart.

Moana agrees.

She will sail!

She will wayfind!

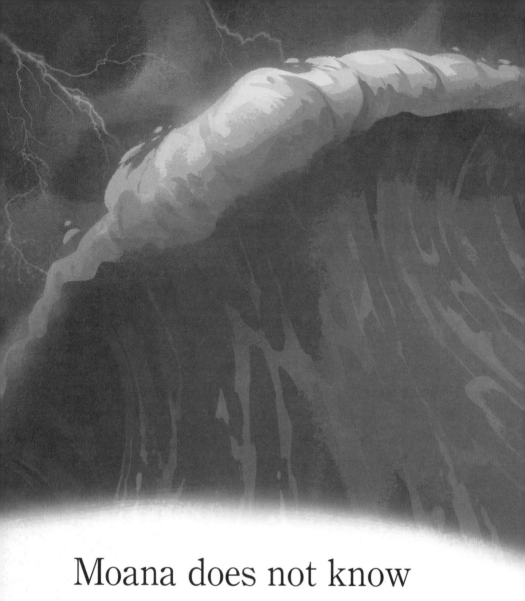

Moana does not know
how to sail.
But she loves the ocean.
She tries to sail.

A storm comes.

Moana is lost.

Moana finds Maui.
Maui does not think
Moana can learn
to wayfind.

He does not want
to help.
The ocean makes
him teach her.

Moana must learn
to use the sun.
She must learn
to feel the waves.

Moana works hard.

She uses the stars.

She feels the waves.

She finds the way!

Monster Te Kā comes.

Big waves rock the boat.

Moana sails fast.

She holds on.

Te Kā is strong.

Moana is smart.

She finds a way.

Moana returns
the heart of Te Fiti.

The darkness leaves.

Plants grow.

Te Fiti blooms.

Life returns
to the islands.

Moana finds her way
back home.
Her family is happy
to see her.

Moana leads her people
to new islands.
She is a great
wayfinder.

She is Moana.

Moana and Pua

adapted by Melissa Lagonegro

based on an original story by Suzanne Francis

illustrated by the Disney Storybook Art Team

Random House 🏠 New York

Moana loves
the ocean.
She dances
in the waves.

Gramma Tala teaches her
all about the ocean.
They love to dance
in the waves together.

Chief Tui has a basket
of piglets.
He needs to bring them
to the farmer.

Moana wants to help.
They will travel
to the other side
of the island.

Chief Tui and Moana
sail with the piglets.
One piglet is not eating.
Moana is worried.

She wants
to help him.
First she must help
steer the boat.

They sail
around the island.
The other piglets
squeal and eat.

But the tiny piglet
is still not eating.
Now Moana is
really worried.

Moana and Chief Tui
reach land.
They jump
into the water.

They pull the boat
to shore.
The tiny piglet watches.

They bring the piglets
to the farmer.
He puts them in a pen.
The tiny piglet
still will not eat.

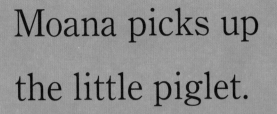

Moana picks up

the little piglet.

Moana fills a leaf
with coconut milk.
She pours the milk
into the piglet's mouth.
He finally eats!

Moana and the piglet
become friends.
She names him Pua.

Moana takes good care
of Pua.

The farmer is glad.

He lets Moana keep Pua.

Moana, Chief Tui, and Pua
go back to the boat.
Moana takes the sail.
She guides them home.

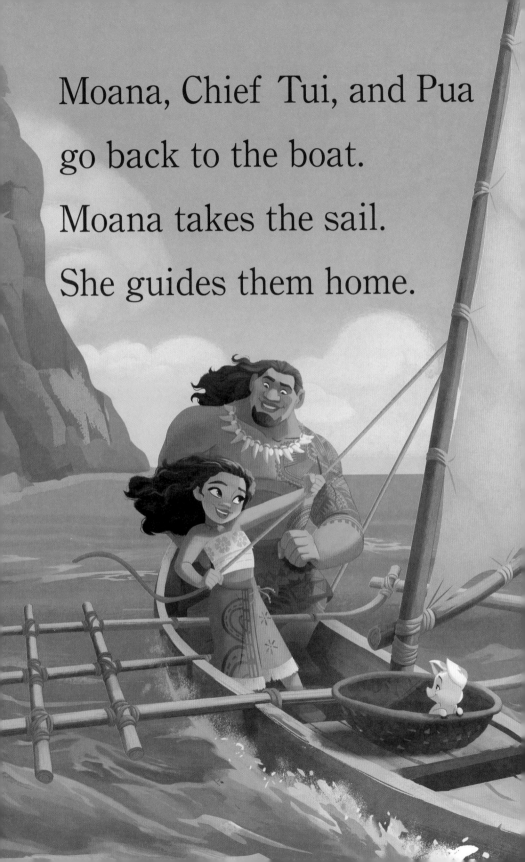

The family watches
Moana care for
her new friend.

Moana feeds Pua.

She keeps him warm.

Moana and Pua play fetch
with coconuts and shells.

They make new friends.

They pretend
to go fishing.
They fill their net
with coconuts.

Moana and Pua
love watching the sunset.
Most of all,
they love being friends!

DISNEY
MOANA

Moana's New Friend

adapted by Jennifer Liberts
based on an original story by Suzanne Francis
illustrated by the Disney Storybook Art Team

Random House 🏠 New York

Moana loves

the ocean!

She loves

to ride the waves

with her pal Pua.

One day,
Moana and Pua meet
a friendly sea turtle.

The sea turtle smiles.

Moana says hello.

The sea turtle loves
to surf!
She stays and plays
all day.

Moana names

her new friend Lolo.

Moana and Pua

say goodbye to Lolo.

Lolo comes back

to play every day.

The friends have fun.
They play games, swim,
and surf.

One night,
Moana and Gramma Tala
look for seashells
on the beach.

Moana sees Lolo crawl
onto the sand.
Lolo digs a hole
by a coconut tree.

Lolo lays eggs in a nest.
There are baby turtles
inside!

When the eggs hatch,
the babies will go
to the ocean.

Each day,

Moana checks the nest.

She hopes to see

the baby turtles hatch.

A big storm comes.
Moana and Pua run home.
The trees bend and sway
in the strong wind.

After the storm,

Moana goes to the beach.

A tree has fallen

on top of the nest!

The turtle eggs
are trapped!
Moana asks her friends
for help.

Moana and her friends
work hard.
Together they move
the tree.

The next day,
the eggs hatch.
The baby turtles
crawl out!

They crawl
to the ocean.
Moana and her friends
protect them.

Moana gives them shade.

Pua chases away a bird.

The baby turtles get

to the water safely!

Moana is so proud!

Lolo's babies are all safe.

They swim and play

in Moana and Lolo's

favorite place—the ocean!

DISNEY

MOANA

Pua and Heihei

adapted by Mary Tillworth

based on an original story by Suzanne Francis

illustrated by the Disney Storybook Art Team

Random House 🏠 New York

It is feast day!

Moana finds a shell.

She will make a gift

for her dad!

Pua the pig

wants to help.

Moana makes
a shell anklet.
She hears a noise.
Heihei the rooster
has a coconut stuck
on his head!

Moana pulls

off the coconut.

Heihei pecks the sand.

Silly rooster!

Villagers get ready
for the feast.
They wrap food
in leaves.
Heihei pecks holes
in the leaves!

A plate sticks
to Heihei's foot.
He is making a mess!
Gramma chases Heihei.

Gramma slips!
Moana catches her.
But the anklet falls
onto Heihei's neck!

Gramma grabs
a basket.
She runs after Heihei.

Gramma traps Heihei
in the basket!
Heihei pecks
the basket.

Gramma will keep Heihei
in the basket
until after the feast.

Moana's anklet is lost!
Pua the pig sees it
in the basket.

Pua will get it back.

He puts the basket

on a stick and jumps.

The basket flies!

But it does not open.

Pua has another idea.
He ties seaweed
around the basket.

Pua runs fast.

The basket bounces.

But it does not open.

Pua tosses the basket
into a tree.
He jumps up
onto a branch.
The branch bends back.

The branch
springs forward.
Pua and the basket fly
through the air!

Pua and the basket land.

Thump!

The basket opens!

Pua and Heihei roll

across the sand.

They roll
into a fishing net.
They are trapped!

The feast begins.

Pua and Heihei roll by.

Moana untangles

the net.

She finds

the anklet!

She hugs Pua.

Moana's dad
loves his gift!
Heihei walks
into the basket again.
Silly rooster!

Disney

MOANA

Quest for the Heart

by Susan Amerikaner

illustrated by the Disney Storybook Art Team

Random House 🏠 New York

Moana lives on an island.

She loves the island.

Most of all,

she loves the ocean.

The island people do not go

beyond the reef.

This is because

of what happened long ago. . . .

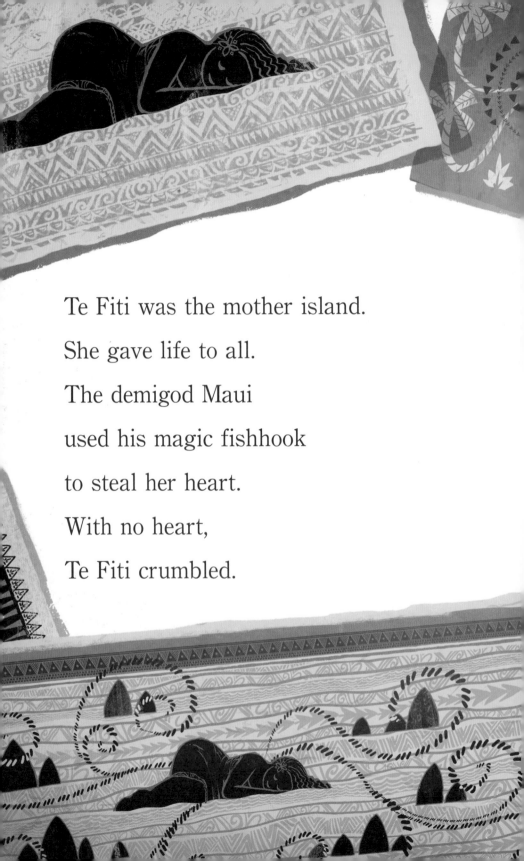

Te Fiti was the mother island.

She gave life to all.

The demigod Maui

used his magic fishhook

to steal her heart.

With no heart,

Te Fiti crumbled.

A terrible darkness spread.
The lava monster Te Kā
struck Maui.
Maui lost his fishhook.
He lost Te Fiti's heart.
Darkness grew.

One day,

the ocean gives Moana

a shiny gift.

It is Te Fiti's heart!

But Moana drops it.

Gramma Tala finds it

and keeps it safe.

Moana grows up.
Her father wants her
to lead her people.
But she is not allowed
to go beyond the reef.

Gramma Tala shows Moana
a secret cave full of old ships.

The island people used to sail
beyond the reef.

They used to be wayfinders!

Gramma Tala gives Moana
the heart of Te Fiti.
She tells Moana to find Maui.
He must return the heart
to Te Fiti.

Moana must sail
beyond the reef.
It is the only way
to save her island.

Moana teaches herself
how to sail.
She sails beyond the reef
into the open ocean.

A storm hits!

The ocean brings Moana

to Maui's island.

Moana meets Maui.

He has many tattoos

that show off his deeds.

Maui thinks he is a hero.

Moana disagrees.

She tells Maui he must return
the heart of Te Fiti.
Maui says no.
He has no power
without his fishhook.

Maui steals Moana's boat.
He sails off without her.
The ocean brings Moana
back to Maui and makes him
teach her to sail.

They must work together
to return Te Fiti's heart.
First, Maui needs to find
his magic fishhook.
Moana will help.

Moana and Maui go
to the world of monsters.
They find a crab monster.
He has Maui's fishhook.
Moana tricks the monster.

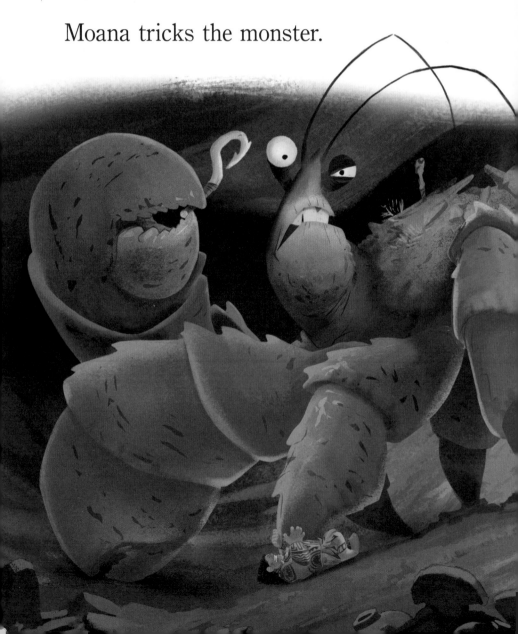

She shows him

a shiny stone.

Maui gets his magic fishhook.

His power is back!

He and Moana escape.

Moana and Maui sail to Te Fiti.

Te Kā blocks their way.

Maui uses his fishhook

to change into a huge hawk.

Te Kā strikes Maui
from the sky.
Moana and Maui
do not give up.

Moana sails fast.

She makes Te Kā angry.

She has an idea.

Moana offers the heart of Te Fiti
to Te Kā.

The heart begins to glow.

Te Kā accepts the heart.

Te Fiti returns.

She blooms with plants.

Life returns to all the islands.

Moana and Maui saved the islands!

They saved each other.

They say goodbye.

They will always be friends.

Maui changes back
into a giant hawk.

Moana returns to her island.

Her parents are happy

she is home.

Maui salutes her.

He is Maui,

the hero.

She is Moana,

the great wayfinder.

She is Moana,

the leader of her people!